BOBBY the BOLD

by **Donna Jo Napoli**
and **Eva Furrow**

illustrated by
Ard Hoyt

Dial Books
for Young Readers

Bobby lived with the chimps at the zoo.

But Bobby was no chimp. He was a bonobo. Bonobos come from the Congo.

Bonobos look like chimps. But chimps are bigger. And bonobos have longer hair. The chimps at the zoo played together and groomed each other. They weren't nice to Bobby, though. They laughed at his hair and they wouldn't groom him.

But people were nice. Sometimes they made funny faces. Sometimes they wore funny clothes. And some groomed their hair in the funniest styles.

The nicest person was the zookeeper. Before she came into Bobby's home, she punched a pretty song on the lock keypad. Before she left, she punched that song again. Bobby liked it.

The zookeeper thought Bobby was smart. She taught him sign language. When he would sign PLAY, she'd let him play zookeeper and wear her jacket. He got so good at helping her make the rounds from animal to animal that she gave him a present: his own little zookeeper jacket.

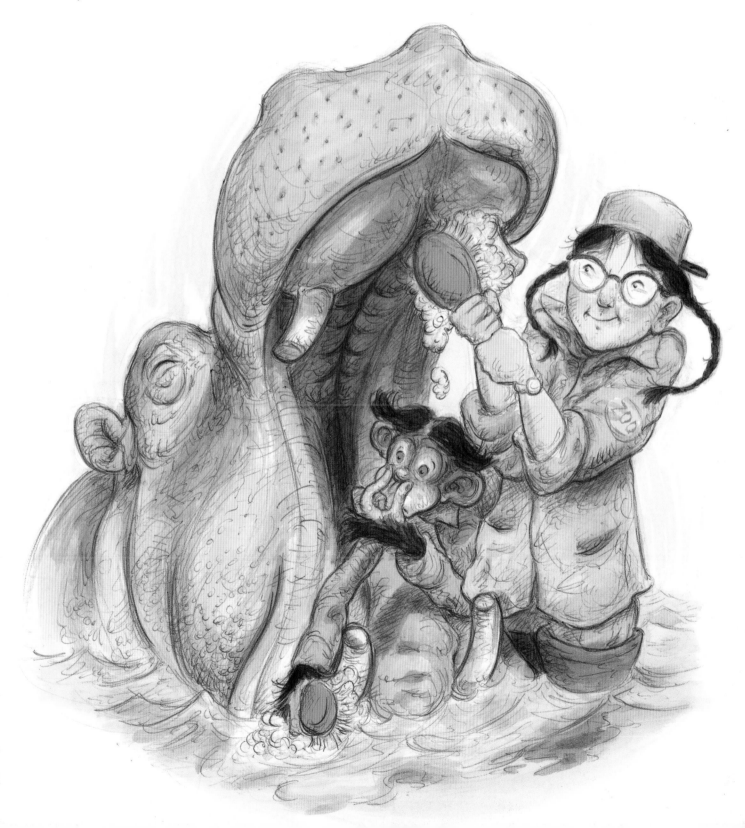

One night after the zoo had closed,
Bobby put on his zookeeper jacket.

Then he punched out the song the zookeeper always
played on the lock keypad. The door opened. Bobby knew
it would. He went out and closed the door behind him.

Bobby waved to the animals. They were surprised. He had never made night rounds before.

When he got to the zoo gate, he climbed over.

Some people were waiting on the corner. Bobby signed PLAY to them, but they didn't seem to understand.

A bus came. The people got in line to get on. Bobby didn't
like waiting in lines. He wiggled in through a window.

"Hey," said a boy. "That zookeeper didn't pay."
"That's no zookeeper. That's a chimp," said a woman, as
Bobby went swinging by. "What's a chimp doing on the bus?"

"Chimps should pay too," said the boy.
Bobby knew the word *chimp*. He signed NOT CHIMP.

A girl on the bus saw him sign. She knew some sign language from her favorite TV program. She asked him in sign who he was.

Bobby signed BOBBY. BONOBO.
The girl said, "He's not a chimp. He's Bobby the bonobo."
"But he didn't pay," said the boy.
"Don't worry about it," said the bus driver. "His teeth are bigger than ours. Let's not make a fuss."

No one else spoke. They just stared at Bobby's big teeth.
So Bobby closed his mouth and did a cartwheel.

The girl giggled.
So Bobby did a backward flip.
Everyone clapped.

As the boy got off the bus, he gave Bobby a pack of gum.
"It's banana," he said. "You'll like it."

That was another word Bobby knew. He signed BANANA.
Then he stuck the gum in his zookeeper jacket pocket.

When the bus passed through the center of town, Bobby got off. He waved to the girl. She waved back. Then everyone else waved too.

Bobby looked in the shop windows. In one shop people were sitting in chairs and grooming each other. They were making funny hairdos.

Bobby went in and took a seat. He looked in the mirror at his fine bonobo face. He spat on his fingers and flattened his hair. What a dashing fellow.

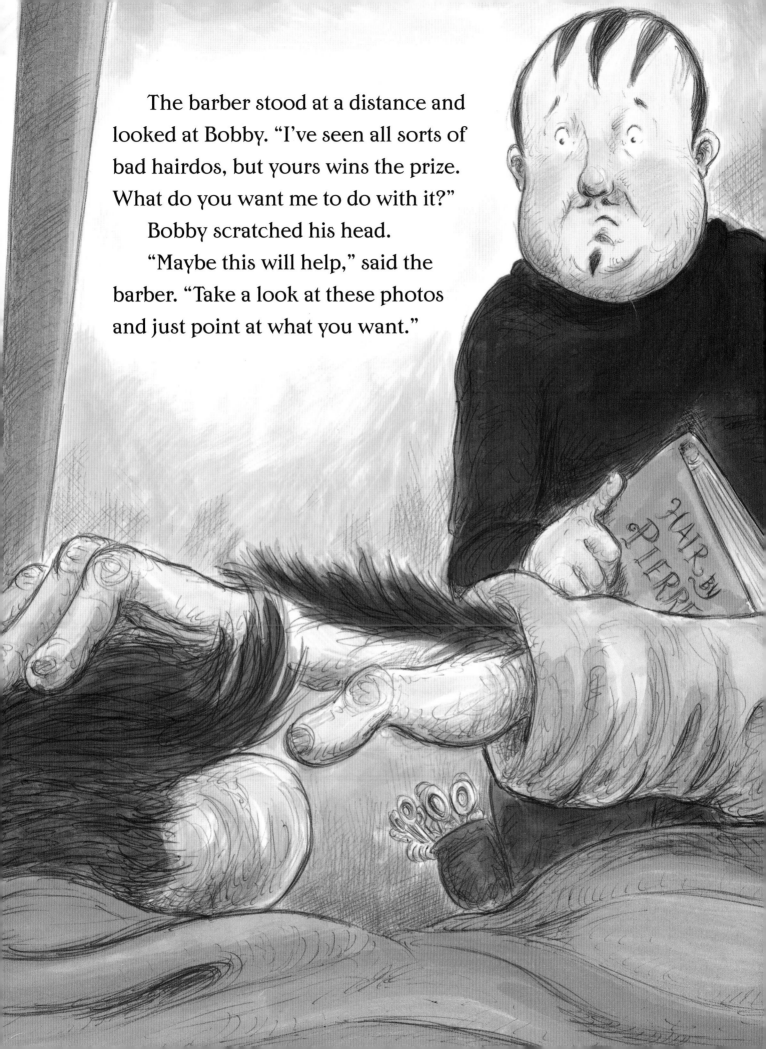

The barber stood at a distance and looked at Bobby. "I've seen all sorts of bad hairdos, but yours wins the prize. What do you want me to do with it?"

Bobby scratched his head.

"Maybe this will help," said the barber. "Take a look at these photos and just point at what you want."

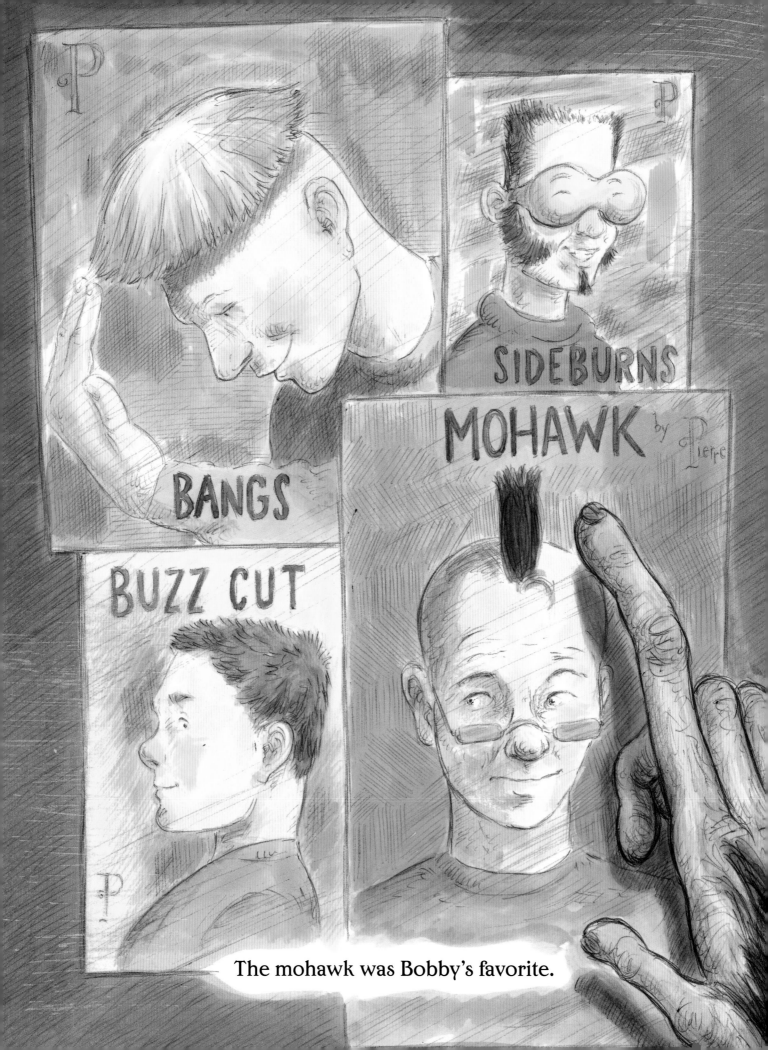

The mohawk was Bobby's favorite.

"You're a bold one," said the barber.
And he cut Bobby's hair into a mohawk.

The gel smelled great. Bobby looked great.

Now it was Bobby's turn to groom the barber. He stood up and pointed at the chair.

"Are you nuts?" said the barber. "I cut my own hair. It's time for you to pay."

Now Bobby was sad.
The barber didn't want to
be groomed.
But Bobby liked his haircut.
So he gave the barber the
pack of gum.

"Banana gum?
Is this what they
chew in the jungle?"
The barber stuck a piece
in his mouth. "Pretty
good." He gave Bobby a
comb and a tube of gel.
"Touch it up every morning."

Bobby went outside and saw a bus going the other direction. The same bus driver sat at the front. So Bobby got on.

"A chimp!" yelped a woman.

"He's not a chimp, he's a bonobo," said the bus driver.

Bobby signed THANKS. Then he did his acrobatic show.

When they got to the zoo, the bus driver stopped. "This is where you get off, Bobby."

Bobby waved to the bus driver
and took his bow. Everyone cheered.

Bobby climbed back over the zoo gate. He went to the primate house and punched the song on the lock keypad. Then he went to sleep.

In the morning, when Bobby opened his eyes, the baby chimps sat in a circle around him. They shrieked in delight.

A baby chimp dunked his head in the pond and tried to shape his hair into a mohawk.

Bobby called him over. He put gel in the baby's hair and formed two horns.

The chimps went crazy over it.
The zookeeper came in.
She signed WOW and HANDSOME.

Bobby did all of their hair.
Everyone was so excited that
they hooted and hugged.

When the chimps settled down, they groomed.
Bobby felt happy in his new spot.
Right in the center.

To the bonobos on the left bank of the Congo River
—D. J. N. and E. F.

To my jewel, Cora, beautiful and bold
—A. H.

DIAL BOOKS FOR YOUNG READERS
A division of Penguin Young Readers Group
Published by The Penguin Group
Penguin Group (USA) Inc., 375 Hudson Street,
New York, NY 10014, U.S.A.
Penguin Group (Canada), 90 Eglinton Avenue East, Suite 700,
Toronto, Ontario, Canada M4P 2Y3
(a division of Pearson Penguin Canada Inc.)
Penguin Books Ltd, 80 Strand, London WC2R 0RL, England
Penguin Ireland, 25 St. Stephen's Green, Dublin 2,
Ireland (a division of Penguin Books Ltd.)
Penguin Books India Pvt Ltd, 11 Community Centre,
Panchsheel Park, New Delhi - 110 017, India
Penguin Group (NZ), Cnr Airborne and Rosedale Roads, Albany,
Auckland, New Zealand (a division of Pearson New Zealand Ltd)
Penguin Books (South Africa) (Pty) Ltd, 24 Sturdee Avenue,
Rosebank, Johannesburg 2196, South Africa
Penguin Books Ltd, Registered Offices: 80 Strand, London WC2R 0RL, England

Text copyright © 2006 by Donna Jo Napoli and Eva Furrow
Illustrations copyright © 2006 by Ard Hoyt
All rights reserved
The publisher does not have any control over and does not assume any
responsibility for author or third-party websites or their content
Designed by Jasmin Rubero
Text set in Edwardian Medium
Manufactured in China on acid-free paper

1 2 3 4 5 6 7 8 9 10

Library of Congress Cataloging-in-Publication Data
Napoli, Donna Jo, date.
Bobby the bold / by Donna Jo Napoli and Eva Furrow ; illustrated by Ard Hoyt.
p. cm.
Summary: Bobby the bonobo is not accepted by the chimps
at the zoo where they all live, but after he has an afternoon adventure in the
city and gets a mohawk hair cut, the chimps change their minds about him.
ISBN 0-8037-2990-1
[1. Bonobo—Fiction. 2. Chimpanzees—Fiction.
3. Hair—Fiction. 4. Zoos—Fiction.]
I. Furrow, Eva. II. Hoyt, Ard, ill. III. Title.
PZ7.N15Bn 2006
[E]—dc22
2005011371